This book belongs to

Andrew

What a Team!

Published by Advance Publishers
www.advance-publishers.com

Written by K. Emily Hutta
Illustrated by Dean Kleven, Adam Devaney, and Yakovetic
Editorial development and management by Bumpy Slide Books
Illustrations produced by Disney Publishing Creative Development
Cover design by Deborah Boone

ISBN: 1-57973-025-6

Princess Atta was trying to study her history lesson, but her little sister, Dot, kept pestering her.

"Aren't you done with that boring old stuff yet?" Dot asked.

"Please stop bugging me, Dot," Atta begged.
"I have lots more to learn before I can be queen
of the anthill."

Just then, Flik appeared at the door.

"Flik!" Dot shouted happily. "I'm so glad you're here. You know how to have fun—not like some big sisters I know."

"I don't have time for fun," Atta sighed.
"Everyone has time for fun," said Flik as he turned
a squealing Dot upside down.

"Actually, I came to see if you two feel like hearing a story," Flik explained.

Atta was tempted. Flik was famous for his stories—full of daring deeds and happy endings. But those were fairy tales, and this was real life. And Atta had a lot of work to do.

"I'm sorry, Flik," Atta said, "but I just don't have time."

"And I don't feel like listening to a story tonight," Dot said. "Let's play make-believe instead!"

"Oh, no, you don't!" Atta said firmly. "It's getting late."

"You never want to do anything fun," Dot complained. "All you want to do is read about the ants that used to live in that spooky old anthill."

"You mean the one on the other side of Ant Island?" Flik asked.

"Yes," replied Atta. "There's a lot we can learn about how ants used to live."

Flik began to look through the leaf scrolls piled on Atta's desk. "Look at this!" he said suddenly.

"What is it?" Dot asked.

"It's a map showing how to get to that old anthill," said Flik.

Dot looked at the mysterious markings on the map. Suddenly Atta's studies didn't seem so boring anymore. "May we go there? May we? Please, please, please?" Dot begged, jumping up and down with excitement.

"I don't think we should," Atta said firmly. "Who knows what we might find?"

"But that's what's so great!" Dot said. "It'll be like a big surprise!"

"Besides, you can't learn everything from a book, Atta," added Flik. "Some things you have to go and find out about for yourself."

"All right," Atta finally agreed. "Let's go tomorrow."

Early the next morning, with the sun barely up, Dot shook her sister Atta awake. "Let's go," she said excitedly. "This is going to be an adventure!"

"That's what I'm afraid of," muttered Atta as she got out of bed.

When Dot and Atta met Flik a little while later, Atta was wearing a backpack.

"What's all that stuff?" Flik asked.

"Supplies," Atta said. "I like to be prepared."

Atta pulled out a map and started leading the others down a trail. But after a few hours, the ants were completely lost.

"How about this way?" asked Flik.

Atta was completely frustrated. "Nothing is where the map said it would be," she said.

"Hmm," said Flik. "Why don't you two wait here while I go ahead and see if I can spot the old anthill? I'll be right back."

"Wait!" called Atta. But Flik was already gone.

Dot and Atta waited and waited, but Flik didn't come back. The sisters began to worry.

"Oh, this is terrible!" Atta cried.

"We'll have to go find Flik," Dot said, climbing a nearby plant to get a better view.

"Dot," said Atta, "come down from there while I figure out what to do!"

"I see the old anthill!" Dot shouted from above.

"But we don't know whether Flik went that way," Atta called up to her. "If we just wait here, maybe Flik will find us again."

"We've waited long enough," Dot said, sliding down the plant. "Flik could be in trouble."

Dot headed off in the direction of the old anthill, and Atta had to hurry to catch up.

The sisters soon found themselves in a thick jungle of plants. Atta got whacked by weeds, and her antennae kept getting tangled up.

Before long, Atta was hot and messy and angry. "So, Dot, is this little adventure still your idea of fun?" she asked.

Just then, the girls heard Flik calling from what sounded like a long way away.

"We're coming, Flik!" Dot shouted, running toward his voice.

"Be careful, Dot!" Atta called after her. But it was too late. Dot had run through a puddle of gooey sap!

As Atta helped Dot clean her feet, Dot looked up at her big sister.

"Thanks," Dot said. "I suppose I should slow down and watch where I'm going."

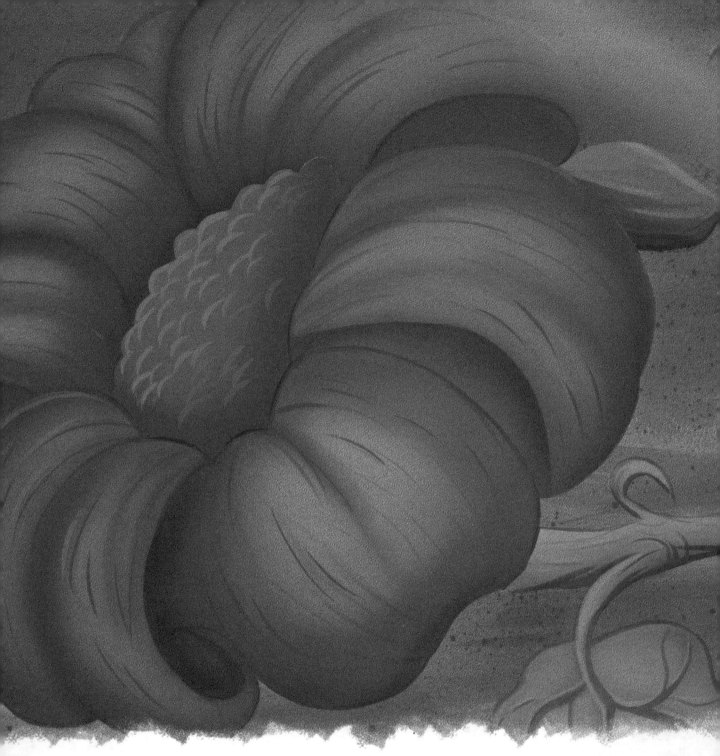

The sisters started on their way again. Suddenly Dot heard a loud rustling overhead. She looked up and saw a bee knock a chunk of pollen over the side of a flower.

"Look out!" Dot shouted. She pushed Atta out of the way just as the pollen thumped to the ground.

"Thanks, Sis," Atta said. "Your quick thinking saved me."

Flik's shouts were louder and closer now, and the girls soon found him. He had slipped into a canyon—and he was stuck there, just out of reach. Dot started to scramble down toward Flik.

"Whoa!" Atta said, holding onto Dot from behind. "If you go down there, we'll have two ants in trouble instead of one."

"What else can we do?" Dot asked.

Atta thought for a minute. "Maybe we can make a rope from that plant over there," she suggested, pointing to a flower.

"Yeah!" exclaimed Dot. "That's a super plan, Atta!"

So Atta and Dot collected the stringy pieces and tied them. Then, together, they hauled Flik up.

Later, the three ants finally found the old anthill. "Wow! Look at that!" exclaimed Flik. "Why don't you two wait here while I go ahead and make sure it's safe?"

But Dot stopped him. "Wait, Flik. Let's stick together and make a plan first," she said and winked at Atta.

Atta smiled at Dot. "That way we can look out for one another," she added.

"Huh?" Flik said.

"Let's just say that today I learned that my little sister is a quick thinker," Atta said proudly.

"And my big sister is a good planner," added Dot.

"Well," said Flik, "you two make quite a team!"

Atta and Dot beamed. They couldn't agree more!

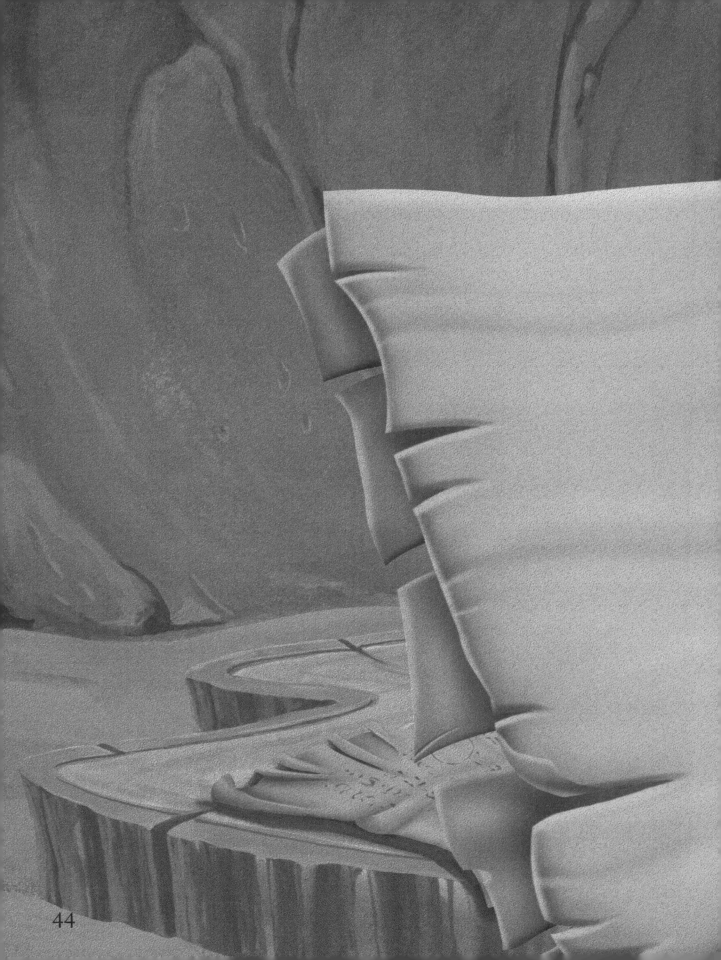

Dear Blueberry Journal,

It used to drive me crazy that Atta was always doing boring stuff like studying. But now I see that she has to do that. It's her special job.

See, all the ants in the colony have jobs they do to help keep the rest of us healthy and happy. Some ants take care of the itsy-bitsy little newborns in the nursery. (They're soooooo cute!) Some gather food or work on the nest. And Atta—well, someday Atta is going to be queen.

I asked my mom what my special job is. She said for now, my job is just growing up!

Till next time,
Dot